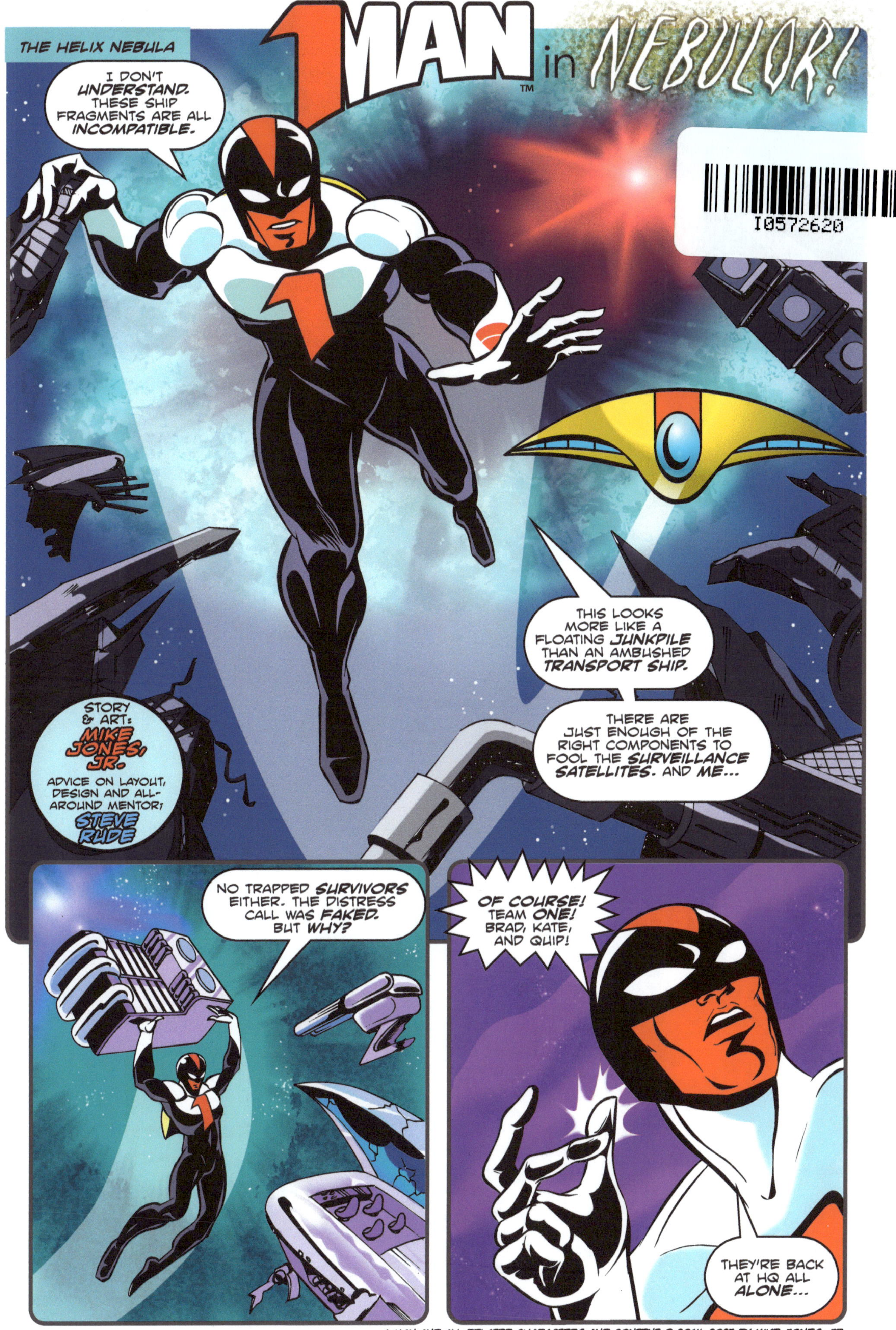
THE HELIX NEBULA
1 MAN in NEBULOR!
I DON'T UNDERSTAND. THESE SHIP FRAGMENTS ARE ALL INCOMPATIBLE.
I0572620
THIS LOOKS MORE LIKE A FLOATING JUNKPILE THAN AN AMBUSHED TRANSPORT SHIP.
THERE ARE JUST ENOUGH OF THE RIGHT COMPONENTS TO FOOL THE SURVEILLANCE SATELLITES. AND ME...
STORY & ART:
MIKE JONES, JR.
ADVICE ON LAYOUT, DESIGN AND ALL-AROUND MENTOR:
STEVE RUDE
NO TRAPPED SURVIVORS EITHER. THE DISTRESS CALL WAS FAKED. BUT WHY?
OF COURSE! TEAM ONE! BRAD, KATE, AND QUIP!
THEY'RE BACK AT HQ ALL ALONE...
1-MAN AND ALL RELATED CHARACTERS AND CONTENT © 2014, 2025 BY MIKE JONES, JR.
1

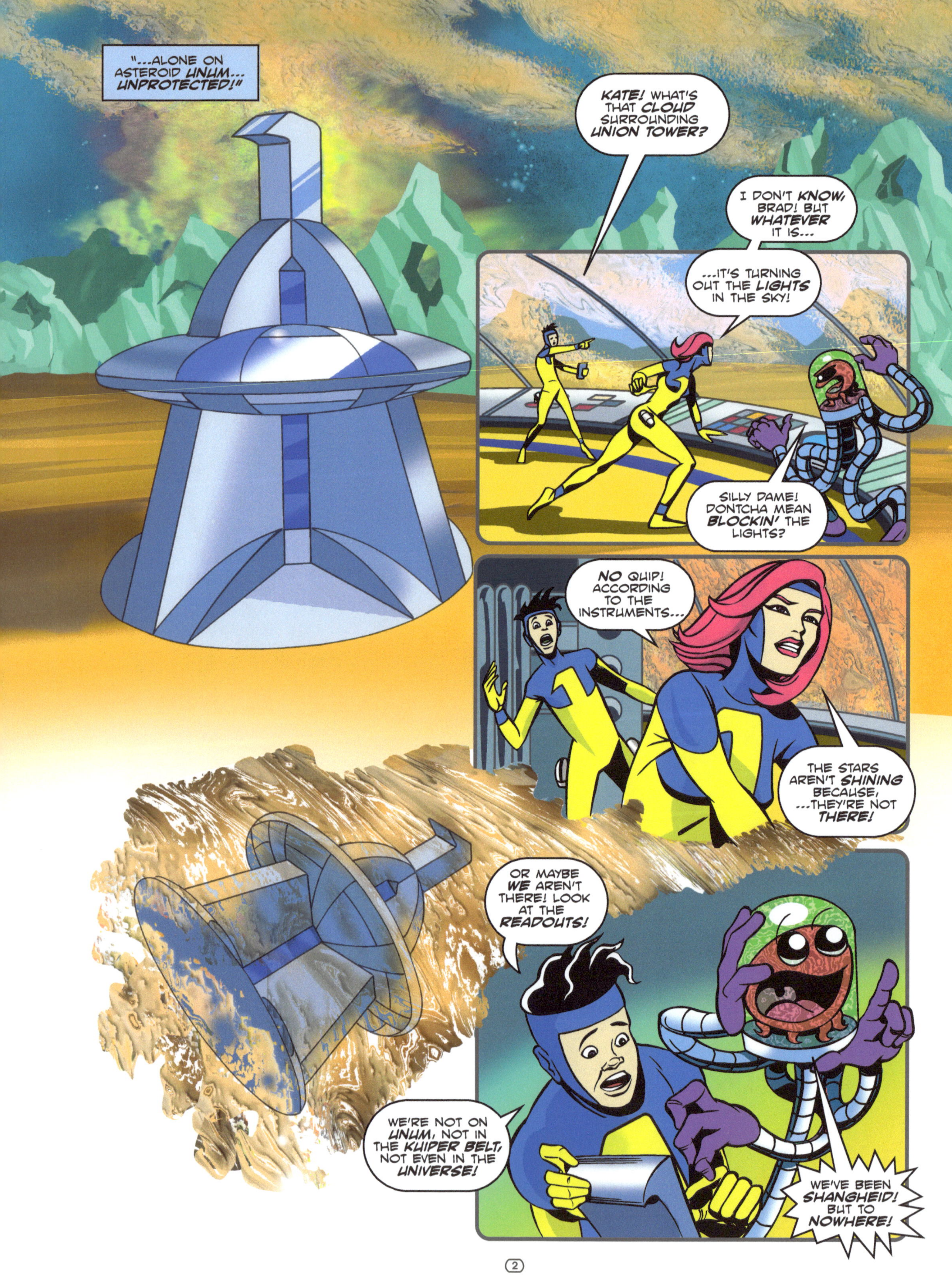

"...ALONE ON ASTEROID UNUM... UNPROTECTED!"
KATE! WHAT'S THAT CLOUD SURROUNDING UNION TOWER?
I DON'T KNOW, BRAD! BUT WHATEVER IT IS...
...IT'S TURNING OUT THE LIGHTS IN THE SKY!
SILLY DAME! DONTCHA MEAN BLOCKIN' THE LIGHTS?
NO QUIP! ACCORDING TO THE INSTRUMENTS...
THE STARS AREN'T SHINING BECAUSE, ...THEY'RE NOT THERE!
OR MAYBE WE AREN'T THERE! LOOK AT THE READOUTS!
WE'RE NOT ON UNUM, NOT IN THE KUIPER BELT, NOT EVEN IN THE UNIVERSE!
WE'VE BEEN SHANGHEID! BUT TO NOWHERE!

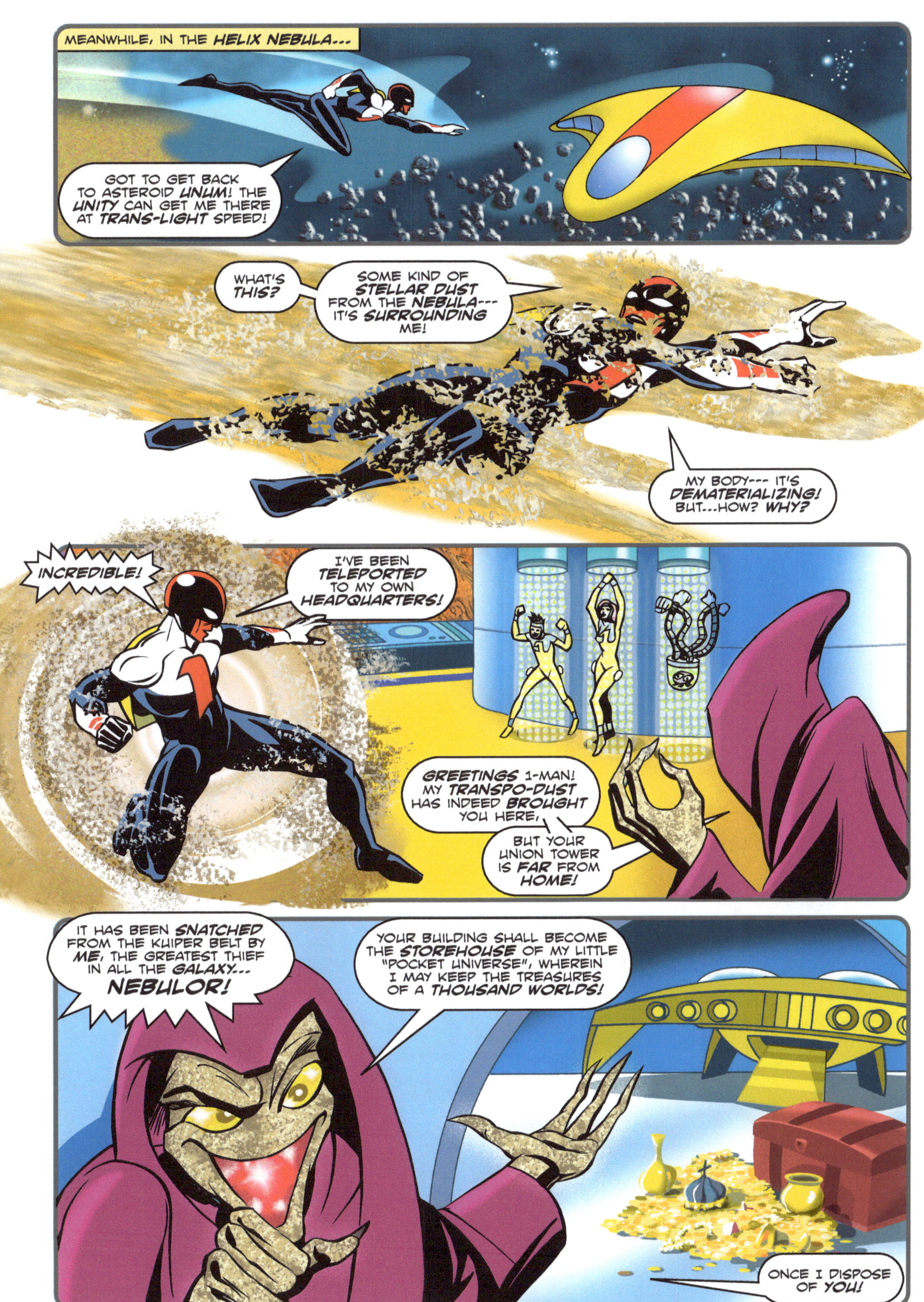

MEANWHILE, IN THE HELIX NEBULA...
GOT TO GET BACK TO ASTEROID UNUM! THE UNITY CAN GET ME THERE AT TRANS-LIGHT SPEED!
WHAT'S THIS?
SOME KIND OF STELLAR DUST FROM THE NEBULA--- IT'S SURROUNDING ME!
MY BODY--- IT'S DEMATERIALIZING! BUT...HOW? WHY?
INCREDIBLE!
I'VE BEEN TELEPORTED TO MY OWN HEADQUARTERS!
GREETINGS 1-MAN! MY TRANSPO-DUST HAS INDEED BROUGHT YOU HERE,
BUT YOUR UNION TOWER IS FAR FROM HOME!
IT HAS BEEN SNATCHED FROM THE KUIPER BELT BY ME, THE GREATEST THIEF IN ALL THE GALAXY... NEBULOR!
YOUR BUILDING SHALL BECOME THE STOREHOUSE OF MY LITTLE "POCKET UNIVERSE", WHEREIN I MAY KEEP THE TREASURES OF A THOUSAND WORLDS!
ONCE I DISPOSE OF YOU!

YOU'RE LIVING IN A DREAMWORLD, NEBULOR!
ATTABOY, 1-MAN!
YEAH! HIT 'IM WIT' YER NEUTRON BLASTS!
ZWEEOOOO!
IMPRESSIVE! YET MY VEIL OF TRANSPO-DUST PROTECTS ME...
SENDING YOUR BLASTS INTO INFINITE SPACE!
THEN I CAN AT LEAST FREE MY FRIENDS!
YEEOW! NOT SO CLOSE!
THAT WILL DO YOU NO GOOD!
WHUMP!
ATTACK! ATTACK MY NEBULONS!
LOOK, 1-MAN! WHAT ARE THEY?
HE CALLED THEM NEBULONS! THEY LOOK LIKE LIVING CLOUDS OF STELLAR DUST!
THAT'S NUTS! HOW CAN DUST HURT US?
LIKE THAT! THEY'RE ABSORBING EVERYTHING THEY TOUCH!
ZWEEOOOO!
THEY'RE REACHING FOR YOU, 1-MAN!

THE NEBULONS ARE FILLING THE WHOLE ROOM! THERE'S NO ESCAPE FROM THEM!
HAVE TO PROJECT MY FORCE FIELD AROUND TEAM ONE!
DON'T DO IT, 1-MAN! YOU'VE GOT TO SHIELD YOURSELF!

NO! THEY'RE ABSORBING HIM!
NOOOOOOOO!
FOOF!

I'M ALL RIGHT, YOU THREE! THEY'VE JUST TRANSPORTED MY ARMS BACK TO THE MILKY WAY.
YES, 1-MAN! WITHOUT YOUR SUIT'S ARMAMENTS YOU'RE HELPLESS!

QUICK! USE YOUR NULL FIELDS, GUYS!
NO, BRAD! I WANT THEM TO SEE US! FOLLOW ME!
I SAW SOMETHING IN THE HANGAR THAT CAN HELP US.

WHAT DID YOU SEE, KATE?
THIS!
NEBULOR'S SPACE SHIP? YOU WANT US TO DESERT 1-MAN?

NO WAY! I AIN'T GONNA DO IT!
OH, PIPE DOWN, QUIP! THAT'S NOT MY IDEA!
WELL WHATEVER YOUR IDEA IS...

...YA BETTER HURRY UP WITH IT!
THOSE NEBULONS ARE TAKING SOME NASTY SHAPES!
HOLD ON! I'M FIRING UP THE SCRAMJET!

THAT BLAST OF WIND!
MY NEBULONS ARE DISSIPATING! THEY'RE UNCONTROLLED!
THEY'RE BLOWING BACK AT ME!
SHOOOSH!!

6

AAAHHHHHHH!!!!!

GOOD WORK, TEAM ONE! MY NEBULONS WERE BLOWN AWAY TOO!
BUT WHERE DID NEBULOR GO?

NO TELLING. HIS OWN CREATURES TRANSPORTED HIM SOMEWHERE FAR AWAY.
HEY LOOK! WITH THE DUST GONE, THE SKY IS COMING BACK!

WE'RE HOME! BACK ON ASTEROID UNUM, ALL IN ONE PIECE!
YOU MEAN ALL EXCEPT FOR ONE PIECE.
HUH? WHADDAYA TALKIN' ABOUT, 1-MAN?
MY SHIP! THE UNITY IS STILL IN THE HELIX NEBULA!
OH BROTHER! THERE'S A LESSON HERE SOMEWHERE!
YEAH! ALWAYS REMEMBER WHERE YOU PARK! HA! HA! HA!
THE END.

# KOMAKK in DEMON BRIDE

WILL YOU HELP US---
AAAAHHH!!!
SO!
INVADE MY DOMAIN WILL YOU? FOOLISH MORTALS!
NO! LAMAKK! LAMAKK!
THE DAUGHTER OF THE CHIEF WILL MAKE A FITTING BRIDE FOR GESHUR, LORD OF THE RIVER DEPTHS!
STOP DEMON!
HAH! A PRIEST OF THE MAKER HAS NO AXE---
ONLY A STAFF! HA! HA! HA! HA! HA!
WHOMM!
TAHNU! SHE IS GONE!
AND LAMAKK IS HURT!
FORGET ME!
CALL... THE MEN.

TANGAR! YOU HAVE COME FOR ME OLD FRIEND. I MUST GO PLEAD WITH THE MAKER FOR TAHNU'S SAFE RETURN.
WHAT ABOUT KOMAKK?
IF THE MAKER HEARS ME...KOMAKK WILL COME.
MINUTES LATER.
WHAT IS WRONG? WHY DO YOU CALL US BACK FROM THE HUNT?
AUROKK! TAHNU HAS BEEN TAKEN BELOW BY GESHUR, THE RIVER DEMON!
AND LAMAKK DID NOT STOP HIM?
HE IS A PRIEST, AUROKK! NOT A WARRIOR.
A PRIEST THE MAKER DOES NOT HEED, IT SEEMS. WHERE IS HE?
IN HIS CAVE, CALLING THE MAKER.
"YOU MEAN HIDING!"
KOMAKK!
STAY HERE, TANGAR! THIS CHALLENGE COMES NOT FROM THE SKIES, BUT FROM THE RIVER DEPTHS.
POWER OF WINDS, CARRY ME ON!
LOOK! IT IS KOMAKK!
CHIEF STYRAKK! WHAT HAS TRANSPIRED?
MY DAUGHTER TAHNU! SHE HAS BEEN SEIZED BY GESHUR THE RIVER DEMON!

THEN WE SHALL BRING THE BATTLE TO THE VILLAIN HIMSELF!
POWER OF WATER, CLEAR A PATH FOR THE MAKER'S MIGHTY MEN!
FOLLOW ME, SEED OF ABEL! THE DEMON SHALL PAY FOR HIS INSOLENCE AT OUR HANDS!
ONLY A FEW CUBITS BELOW AND WE ARE AT THE DEMON'S DOORSTEP!
TO THINK THAT HE HAS BEEN SO NEAR, BIDING HIS TIME!
HIS TIME HAS ENDED! WE SHALL SEE TO THAT!
KOMAKK, LOOK!
SERPENTS BY THE LEGION! COULD THEY...?
PENETRATE OUR BUBBLE? OF COURSE! THEY ARE AIR BREATHERS!
UNNHH!—I CAN—WITHSTAND THEIR WOUNDS,—BUT THESE MEN CANNOT! I MUST SAVE THEM!
THERE ARE TOO MANY! AXES ALONE WILL NOT STOP THEM!

POWER OF WINDS, RETURN MY COMRADES TO THE SURFACE!
NO, KOMAKK! I WILL NOT ABANDON TAHNU!

I WOULD SEE THIS THROUGH TO THE END!
AS YOU WISH, AUROKK!
WE SHALL FOLLOW THE SERPENTS TO THE DEMON'S LAIR!

AND IN THE GROTTO OF GESHUR...
WHAT'S THIS? INVADERS! SET UPON STEALING MY BRIDE, I SEE!
SHE IS NO BRIDE OF YOURS, DEMON!

POWER OF EARTH, BE MY STRENGTH!
YOU HAVE NEVER WITNESSED STRENGTH, HUMAN PUP!

WHOOM!
HUMAN I MAY BE, DEMON...
BUT HUMAN AS THE MAKER FIRST INTENDED...
...FULL OF HIS POWER!
ZZHHAAPP!

THOOM!
TAHNU!

FEAR NOT, KOMAKK! I HAVE HER!
I MUST END THIS QUICKLY IF YOU TWO ARE TO SURVIVE.
POWER OF FIRE!

BURN WITH HEAVEN'S LIGHT!
AAARRGGHH!!

HE IS GONE!
RETURNED TO THE LOWER DEPTHS, BUT MY POWER IS NEARLY SPENT.
I WILL SEND YOU TO THE SURFACE.

AND IN THE EXILE VILLAGE...
TAHNU! IS SHE...?
FATHER!
SHE IS WELL, MY CHIEF.
TAHNU! SHE IS SAFE?

KOMAKK RAN INTO SOME TROUBLE WITH GESHUR...
BUT I WAS ABLE TO RESCUE TAHNU.
THANKS... BE TO YOU, AUROKK!
YES, LAMAKK. YOUR CALLINGS TO THE MAKER WERE INDEED HEARD.

I LIVE TO SERVE MY CHIEF AND ALL HIS FAMILY.
AUROKK...
TO HAVE THAT GAZE FOCUSED IN MY DIRECTION I WOULD GIVE MY LIFE.
BUT I DARE NOT SPEAK.

NO MATTER WHAT THE COST.
THE END.

# THE MERCURIONS™ IN THE MEKKANOIDS!

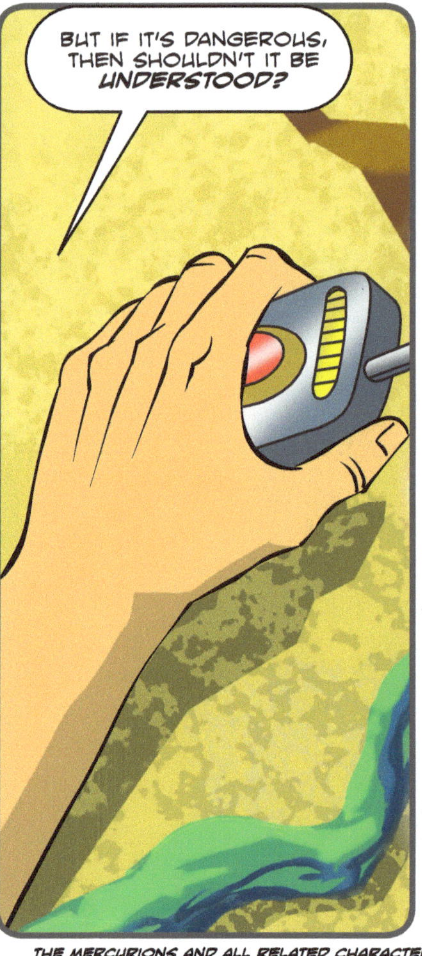

Continued on 3rd page following

# From whence cometh the Omni-Men ?

by MIKE JONES, JR.

The Saturday morning television season of 1967 will, in my mind, probably never be equaled. The animated series **1-Man and Dino-Sara** had debuted the previous year, blasting open my 4-year-old imagination like nothing before it. I *loved* the show, and would never have dared to hope for more. Yet incredibly, the next year there *were* more shows added to satisfy the growing demand for pulse-pounding, adrenaline-pumping, animated entertainment. There were **The Mercurions**, a human family on a far-distant planet, fighting for survival in a primitive and dangerous world. There was **Komakk, in the Valley of the Exiles**, a stone-age superhero in combat against prehistoric monsters and demons in Earth's distant past. **Alan Kazamm** offered mystical adventure in a land of magic, and **Nimrod, the Hunter** was a legendary-figure-as-superhero who fought supervillains in our own time, as did **Icarus, the Man-Bird.** Not to exclude any possible vista for heroic narrative, **Seawolf, the Super Whale** was created to keep even the high seas safe from malevolent beings. And to see if lightning could indeed strike twice, **The Galactics** were produced as a team of space-faring superheroes who fought tyranny among the planets in a manner similar to *1-Man*. Amazingly, these series were all the product of one company; *Big Hit Cartoons*.

In the 1950's, Oscar-winning animators Bill Banner and Joe Herrera pioneered the effort to create low budget television animation, mostly of the funny animal variety, and met with great success. Yet their first attempt at serious action storylines in 1964, the prime-time series **Project A.P.E.X.**, was cancelled after only one season due to its expensive nature. But reruns proved the team of globe-hopping adventurers never truly left the hearts and minds of sixties' youths, nor that of Joe Herrera.

In 1966 Joe made another go at serious adventure, this time for Saturday morning. He contacted Alex Huth, well-known comic book artist of the 1950's, to help him craft a new superhero for television. The co-creation of Joe and Alex, *1-Man* had an enormous impact on that television season. For the first time, young boys were staying home to watch television on Saturdays instead of going outside to play. The die had been cast, and the directive from television producers of all three networks was "Make me a show like *1-Man!*"

Ironically, the company most successful at creating competition for *1-Man* was *Big Hit Cartoons* itself. In 1967, BH produced superhero shows for all three networks, often competing in the same time slots! For the next year and a half our little black and white RCA set introduced me to the menaces of Lizard Men, Muck Men, Fire Men, and Snake Men! There were monsters, mad scientists, and intergalactic raiders, with names like Proteus, Tesserak, and Zongar! But most of all, there were *heroes;* selfless individuals who prized the life and liberty of others over themselves. Heroes who wore cool outfits, had dramatic abilities and liked to shout their own names! Add to that some truly stirring music and the concoction was irresistable!



16

Yet events soon began to transpire that I didn't comprehend at the time. In 1968 Dr. Martin Luther King, Jr. and Senator Robert Kennedy were killed by assassins' bullets. Somehow my heroes were being blamed for it. Within a few months they had disappeared from the airwaves, replaced by the likes of **Sleuth Mutt** and **Heidi and the Hepcats.** The reason given? "Violence", which became the new naughty word of the media and parents' watchdog groups. This was the word they used to describe action, drama, suspense, and *fun!* The televised forays into imagination and bravery, which actually inspired me to be a *better* kid, were soon yanked off television to placate the naysayers. They would sometimes reappear in reruns as the new shows would fail (no surprise to me, even then). Yet by the Fall TV season of 1970 my heroes had been taken away from Saturday morning forever.

I was an adult when I next saw these shows, thanks to the advent of videotape. While *A.P.E.X.* and *1-Man* largely held up to the test of time, I was disappointed in the rest. Though they had much more style than cartoons produced by other animation companies of the day (thanks to Alex Huth's designs and some great jazzy music), I found that the plots and characterizations were lacking and formulaic, and I had many questions about the premises that were not satisfactorily answered. Most of the heroes weren't even given origin stories. I soon decided that I wanted to rectify all that. I wanted to create a logic for all their situations. And I wanted to tell how they all came to *be.*

Two years ago I scored a meeting at an Arlington comic-con with Don Didymus, publisher of PC comics (current owners of the characters). I shared with him an origin pitch for *Komakk* which he liked, and he asked if I wanted to tackle any more of the BH group of 60's heroes. I told him that I wanted to do them ALL. And I wanted all the characters to MEET and fight a common threat. When I explained this to Don, he was somewhat taken aback.

You see, one of BH's shows of 1967 was Dan Smee and Mack Derby's superhero team **The Moleculoids,** published by *Wonder Comics Group.* This threw a significant monkey wrench into the proceedings, as Wonder Comics and PC are fierce publishing rivals! When Don objected, I responded, "Oh, well I want to use the *Locust* also". At this point, Don nearly threw his coffee mug at me. **The Locust,** of course, is Wonder's hottest property, and the wall-crawling crime-fighter is the subject of many blockbuster movies.

"Why the *Locust,* fer gosh sakes?" Don bellowed. "BH didn't even *do* that series!" My response was that even though *The Locust* was not a BH series, his presence was so powerful in the TV landscape of 1967 that I felt he was in the same world and had to be included. "You're *crazy,* Jones! Absolutely *crazy!*" Don said, but I noticed that he quickly went in search of Wonder head publisher Joe Quixotta.

The rights negotiations turned into the most legally complex since Roger Rabbit, but it was all worth it. Your eyes now behold the beginnings of a tale which will bring together heroes from different times, different planets, different dimensions, three networks, two animation companies, and two publishers! It is an illustrious group that could only be called, **"The Omni-Men!"** Book One will establish the worlds of these characters for the uninitiated. Then *six more* volumes will take you from the distant past, to the far future and back again, with ALL these characters along for the ride! *Don't miss it!*

P.S. *Don't tell Don that I also snuck in cameos of the 1966* **Wonder Super Heroes** *show characters. He still hasn't paid the* **last** *licensing fee!*



| TV GRID | 9:00 | 9:30 | 10:00 | 10:30 |
| September 9, 1967 | | | Central Time | |
| --- | --- | --- | --- | --- |
| and Friends | Flintrocks | Nimrod the Hunter | Icarus and the Galactics | Atomic Aphid/ Secret Sloth |
| urions | Alan Kazamm | 1-Man and Dino Sara | Komakk and Sea Wolf | Superion/Aquarion Hour of Adventure |
| culoids | The Locust | 20,000 Leagues Under the Sea | Wonder Super Heroes | Melvin of the Apes |

JONGLIN! PUT THAT THING DOWN!
AJOR!
THOOM!
SOMETHING HAS BEEN UNEARTHED! SOMETHING EVIL!
I'M SORRY, FATHER.
MEKKANOIDS! AND THEY'RE PREPARING TO FIRE!
NO WORRIES, FATHER! WE HAVE YOU COVERED!
ZUMM!
ZUMM!
ZUMM!
ZUMM!
ZUMM!
SCOTTIE! SHE'S BROUGHT DEKE AND WALLY!

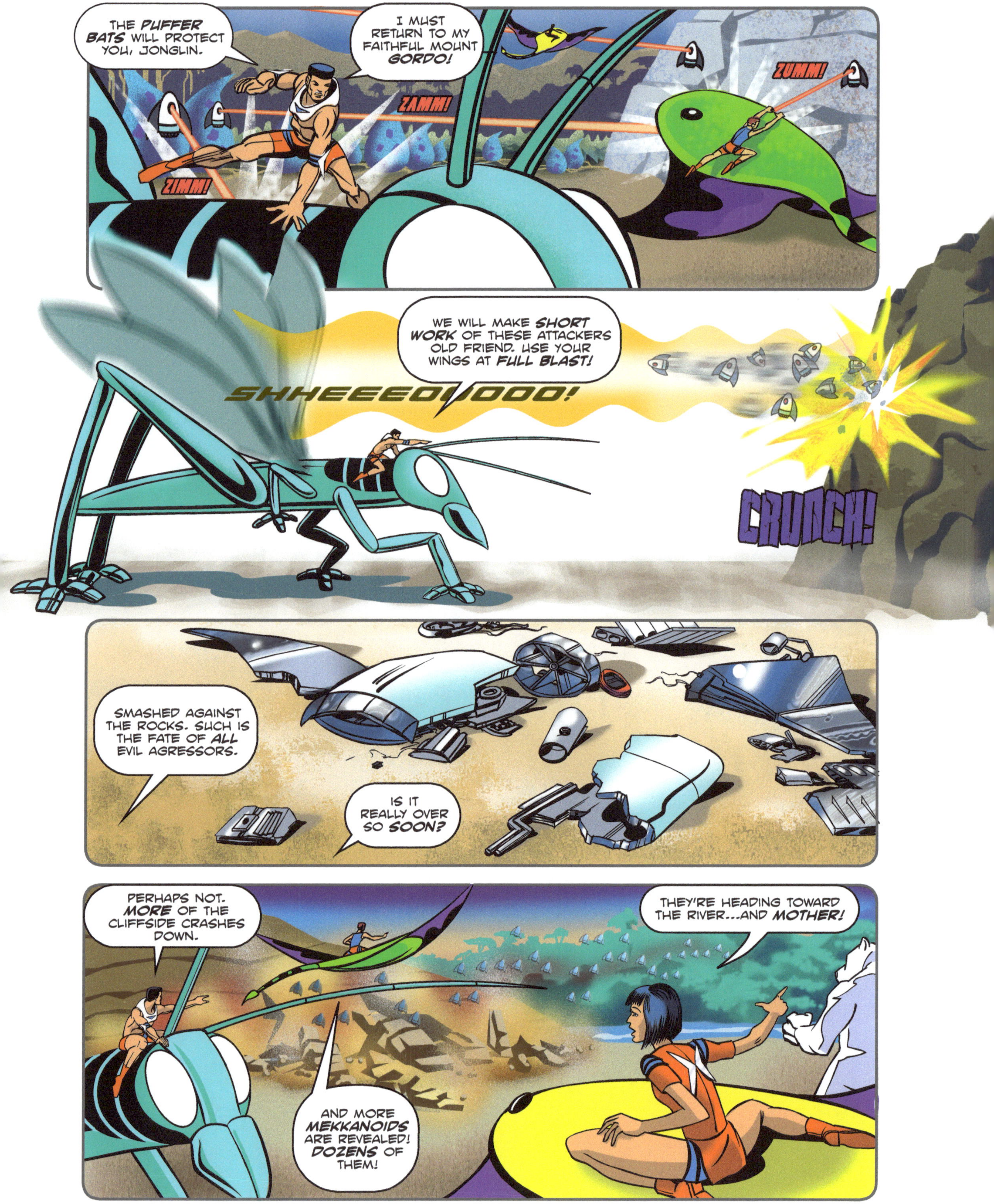

THE PUFFER BATS WILL PROTECT YOU, JONGLIN.
I MUST RETURN TO MY FAITHFUL MOUNT GORDO!
ZIMM!
ZAMM!
ZUMM!
WE WILL MAKE SHORT WORK OF THESE ATTACKERS OLD FRIEND. USE YOUR WINGS AT FULL BLAST!
SHHEEEOUOOO!
CRUNCH!
SMASHED AGAINST THE ROCKS. SUCH IS THE FATE OF ALL EVIL AGRESSORS.
IS IT REALLY OVER SO SOON?
PERHAPS NOT. MORE OF THE CLIFFSIDE CRASHES DOWN.
AND MORE MEKKANOIDS ARE REVEALED! DOZENS OF THEM!
THEY'RE HEADING TOWARD THE RIVER...AND MOTHER!

HERE THEY COME, SHEP. USE YOUR SONIC VIBRATIONS TO LURE THEM INTO THE NET.
WOOPWOOPWOOPWOOPWOOPWOOPWOOP
THAT SHOULD BE PLENTY. THANKS, SHEP!
THESE WILL MAKE A FINE DINNER IF AJOR DOESN'T BURN THEM.
WHAT'S THAT NOISE? SOMETHING'S COMING THROUGH THE TREES!
IT'S SOME KIND OF MEKKANOID! IT'S GOING TO FIRE!
KLAAANNNGGG!!!

UH OH.
MERCURIONS! TO GEMNEE'S SIDE, QUICKLY!
SMASH!
ZIMM!
AJOR!
KA-ZAPF!
ZUMM!
ZAMM!
ATTACK! DESTROY THE MEKKANOIDS!
KRRRONCH!

FATHER! WALLY'S FLYING THE CRISS-CROSS MANUEVER ALL BY HIMSELF!
WHERE ARE JONGLIN AND DEKE?
ZAMM!
BRRZAPP!

KA-ZING!
WERE THEY NOT BEHIND US?
KA-ZASK!

THAT BOY IS IN SO MUCH TROUBLE!
ZUMM!
WOOPWOOPWOOPWOOPWOOPWOOPWOOPWOOPWOOP

AJOR! GEMNEE! SCOTTIE!
I HAVE THE ANSWER!
JONGLIN!

THAT DEVICE HAS CAUSED ENOUGH HARM! FIRE ON IT, GEMNEE!
NO, MOTHER! THE DEVICE IS THE KEY!
AIM SHEP'S POWER INTO THE DEVICE, BUT DON'T DESTROY IT!
WOOPWOOPWOOPWOOPWOOPWOOPWOOP
THAT'S IT, SHEP! YOUR SMALLEST BEAM, AT FULL FORCE!
SOMETHING'S HAPPENING! IT'S DISCHARGING BLASTS!
SHEP'S POWER WAS RELAYED BACK THROUGH THE DEVICE. IT WAS TOO MUCH FOR THEM!
THEY'RE DESTROYED!
FFRZttt!
THREATENED BY TEKNOL AND SAVED BY TEKNOL!
WE'RE ONLY SAFE FOR THE TIME BEING.
INDEED. SOMEONE IS BEHIND THESE MEKKANOID ATTACKS.
SOMEONE WHO WILL FACE THE FULL MIGHT OF THE MERCURIONS!
RRAAWWR!
THE END.

# THE SCHOOL

## (in which Steve Rude gives me a comics critique)

I know what you're thinking. How did a guy you've never heard of end up getting professional comics assistance from one of the greatest living comics artists of the day? Well, it was sort of the equivalent of "starting out in the mailroom". In 2006 I won a contest to become **Rude Dude Productions** graphic designer by producing the winning logo. Since then I have laid out his comics and graphic novels, sketchbooks, and also helped out with Steve's coffee table book **Artist in Motion**. Steve has even let me do some typographic embellishments for his **Dark Horse Presents** Nexus work and for the **Before Watchmen** Dollar Bill story (for which I did the newspaper graphics. Woo hoo!)

During work on the **Artist in Motion** book, Steve came out to stay with me for an intense couple of weekends to finish off that monster. During his second visit he also found time to offer a painting demo at Hardin-Simmons University here in Abilene, TX where I teach graphic design, and we quickly formed a bond. Being around Steve was immensely inspiring, as I found that he loved so many of the same things I did; Jonny Quest and the Alex Toth-designed superhero cartoons of our youth, Jack Kirby, John Romita Sr., the sci-fi TV shows of the 60's, etc. The Dude's sketchbooks were full of drawings done from old animation model sheets and TV freeze frames, and yet he was a real artist; an illustrator and painter of worldwide reknown. Steve was successful, yet had never abandoned his childhood passions and was unashamed of them. In this way Steve's example gave me

## STORYTELLING

Steve's redo of Tahnu.

My recreation of it.

**KOMAKK, Panel 1**

When Steve saw this first panel his reaction was, "Okay, this is nice, this is perfectly.... adequate...". And then he proceeded to thoughtfully sketch as he started asking me questions about the characters, such as "Who is this guy (Lamakk)? What is he about? Who is she (Tahnu)? How do they feel about each other?". As I elaborated on Lamakk as a priest with the secret identity of a superhero who was in love with the chief's daughter, he continued to sketch and came up with the following advice;

"She likes him. I can tell. But she doesn't want to admit it. She wants to make him sweat. If she is the main love interest you've got to make her more alluring, more beautiful, and more 'come hither' than the other girls. You've gotta have that." And he proceeded to create a more tantalizing pose for her, which I emulated.

Then Steve talked about Lamakk's facial expression. He is on "guard duty" over the women while the men are hunting

(yes, I know how old-school and sexist this all sounds. But don't forget that both Kate and Gemnee save the day in this issue!)

You can see how stiff Lamakk is, which became instantly obvious as soon as I saw Steve's reinventions. My thoughts were that Lamakk was guarded and trying to seem nonchalant, but it just comes across as stiff when you see these great alternatives Steve did. He stressed how poses should mirror the

# OF DUDE

## By Mike Jones, Jr.

"permission" to go ahead and create my Omni-Men project, as I realized it was "okay" for me to still love the things I did when I was 8 yrs. old!

There was just one problem. I wasn't ready. When I saw in person the way Steve attacked his comics projects and art studies with such a fanatical work ethic and dedication, I was ashamed. I had longed to be a cartoonist since I first saw a Sunday comics section and had dabbled in it all my life. But decades of "playing it safe" in the art world as a graphic designer meant decades of not doing enough comics. I needed help. I needed a mentor.

Lucky for me, I knew Steve Rude! Thanks to him I have dared to dust off the fascinations of childhood and dreams long-deferred. Steve has helped me immensely by critiquing my comics work, and I hope these insights will also benefit others. I may eventually turn these notes into a book with which The Dude and I will sell millions of copies and make out like bandits, but for now I'm just trying to remember it all! Also, I thought you might find it interesting to see just what my mentor is doing for me. So here goes.....!

▲ The Dude creates posing options for Lamakk. ▶

characters thoughts and force the viewer to make a judgment, so I chose the one at bottom right, which kept a guardedness, but revealed Lamakk's interest in Tahnu.

### KOMAKK, Panel 2

At top right you can see my original pencils for panel 2. Steve wanted to demonstrate to me how endless the posing possibilities are. His 6 variations are beneath my panel. I ended up doing no. 3, as I didn't want Lamakk to seem too relaxed, but I did want to eliminate his stiffness.

KOMAKK, Panel 3

© 2012 Steve Rude

*The Dude gets us inside Lamakk's head.*

On the last panel of the first page, I humbly bring you.... *more stiffness!* The Dude proclaimed about my drawing of Lamakk's face, "This tells me nothing. I have no idea what this guy is thinking." Once again I was relying on subtlety and the dialogue to get the meaning across, but Steve wanted me to get the meaning across with NO WORDS. If you can understand the basic actions without the dialogue, he said, you know you're doing your job as a cartoonist.

Steve began experimenting with different facial expressions for Lamakk and I saw how fun that could be. My final result was probably still too subtle, but its just a personal trait I'll have to work against.



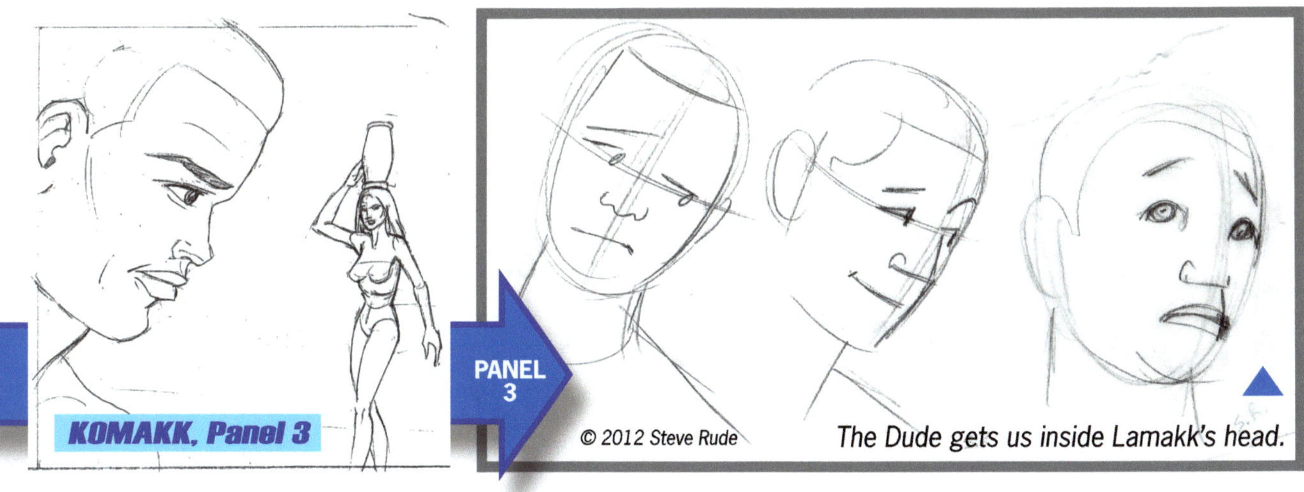

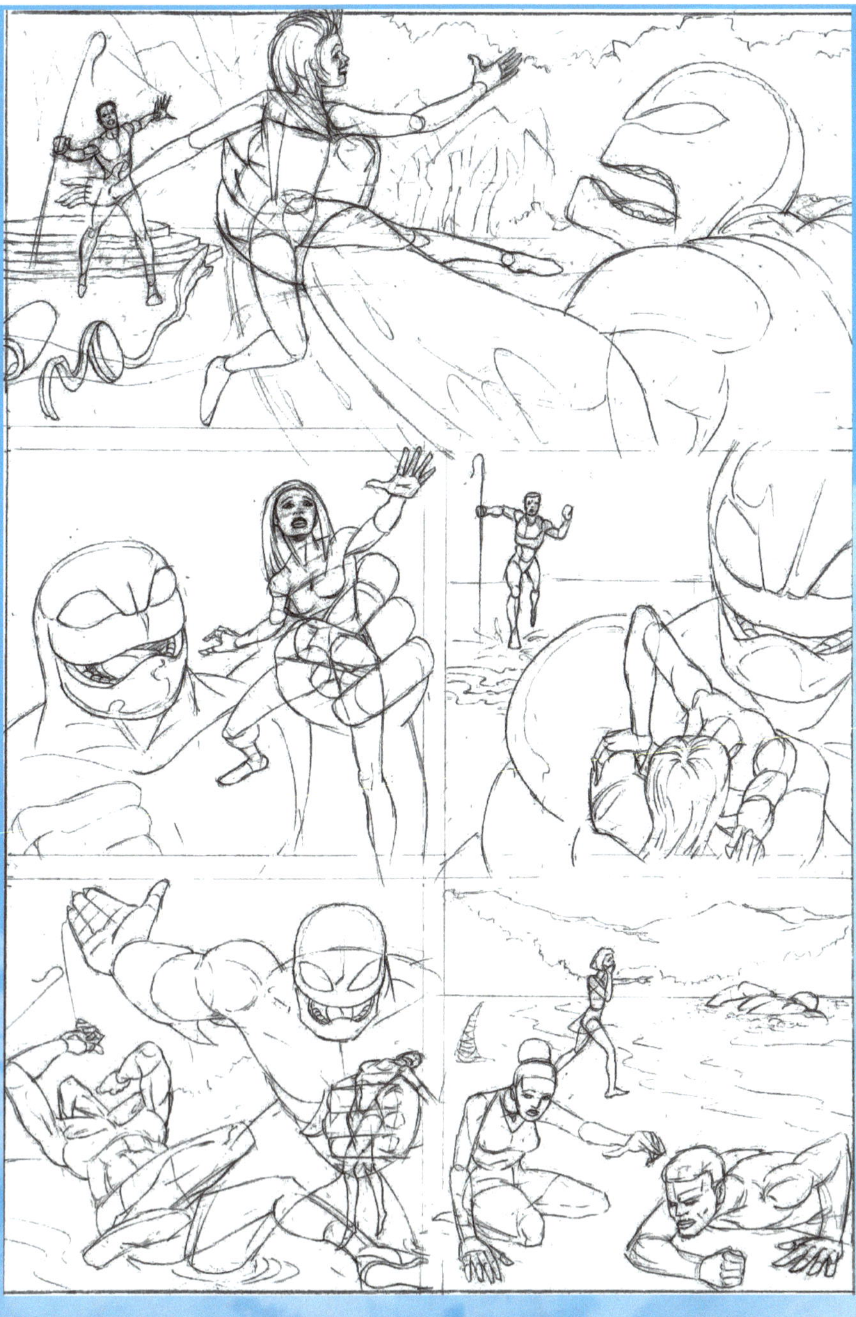

## KOMAKK, Page 2

This page started out quite differently, as you can see at left. It had several problems, most glaring of which was the first panel. At the end of page 1, you have no hint that there is any kind of menacing character anywhere around. Then all of a sudden at the top of page 2, Tahnu has been grabbed by this giant river creature. There is no set-up, or "establishing shot" as they say in the biz. I was actually aware of this shortcoming before Steve saw it, but I was so enamored of my drawing and mindful of my limited space of 7 pages, I figured I *had* to do it this way. That's where another pair of eyes can talk you down from the ledge and bring you back to sanity. Establishing shots really *are* necessary.

*The original pencils for Page 2. No establishing shot in the first panel, panel 2 is extraneous, the action is unclear in panel 4, and Shayna has too passive a pose in panel 5.*

Steve produced a quick 2" thumbnail sketch for a new page layout. It establishes the creature appearing and the shock of the villagers. In his new panel #2, he showcases the "grab" of Tahnu. Also, since we haven't seen Geshur's face yet, panel 3 becomes the intro of his frightening visage. This delay in the reveal adds drama, as my original version had his face shown in all 3 of the first panels. Another basic principle not to be skipped; *preliminary thumbnail layouts!*

Now comes panel 4. I had drawn a pose of Lamakk being backhanded by Geshur and I liked the poses they were in...
...until Steve did this.

With the straightness of Geshur's striking arm and the obvious position of the powerless Lamakk, the message again became crystal clear. CLARITY! My original poses might have been more Baroque, with their turning and twisting and drama, but they weren't as clear. In my original version, did Geshur just slap him on the back or what? Is Lamakk trying to jump up to his arm? Who knows? Obviously, the Dude had just "schooled". In these matters, Steve defers to the approach of Abilene born (*koff* *koff*) cartooning great of the 30's and 40's, Roy Crane.

On the last panel you can see how Steve added drama to the pose of Shayna by stretching her out to reach for Lamakk and adding more concern to her face. This shows yet again the need for communicating without words. Pantomime is the key to good cartooning.

# STORYTELLING

## KOMAKK, Page 3

**S**teve made no comments about this initial version of page 3 of Komakk. He simply began sketching the fantastic drawings you see at right. I marveled at what he had done and decided to change quite a bit about the page.

First, I couldn't believe that I had shown before and after poses (panels 1 and 2), yet skipped the actual dramatic moment when Shayna blows the alarm horn. Again I thought I had no space for it, but after seeing Steve's drawing, I knew I couldn't omit that. Also, his pose of Lamakk kneeling was much more profound than mine.

Finally, Komakk's transformation panel had infinitely greater impact with its upward thrust and backward arch. I knew I had to make it the focal point of the layout with a really large panel. Yet where would the space come from?

As you can see in the book, I simply made panels 1 and 2 skinny and horizontal and totally deleted panel 6 where Komakk is flying out of the cave.

This page, perhaps more than any other, taught me not to miss the best moments. As Joe Barbera once said, "Why ignore the obvious?"



Shayna blows the horn. Don't skip the dramatic moments!

© 2012 Steve Rude

Are your poses as emphatic and clear about the character's attitude as they can be?

© 2012 Steve Rude

Don't ignore the obvious!

© 2012 Steve Rude

The particular appearance of a character can make or break its effectiveness. Steve felt my original chief design was too plain (you can see him with a wolf cowl opposite). The Dude then gave me the wonderful sketch you see above, emphasizing that a chieftain should seem special and be more ornate than the other tribesmen. So Steve did an elaborate feathered headress.

This greatly inspired me, and I did my own version at right, but decided to make the headress more in line with the dinosaur theme. I did this by changing the feathers to a styracosaurus skull, which accomplished the goal and kept the same spirit as Steve's.

The design of Geshur also changed considerably from my first penciled page to the final product. My initial thought was that he be like a river eel, and so my design reflected that. Again, Steve championed the need for clarity and stated that Geshur should have the trappings that would make him more obviously a creature of water, such as fins, spikes, etc. Below is Steve's version, and of course you can see how I incorporated some of those concepts in the finished pages.

© 2012 Steve Rude

© 2012 Steve Rude

© 2012 Steve Rude

At one point Komakk had a Loki-like ponytail and I also drew a version with dreadlocks, but abandoned them because that was such an unlikely look for a 60's cartoon show. Yet when Steve made his vast improvement of my pose at top left (by pointing Komakk more toward the viewer and opening his mouth more dramatically) he intuitively added hair which became dreadlocks. He told me I shouldn't worry too much about what was likely in the 60's and go with what was right for the character. I was pretty pleased that my initial instincts had been validated!

Below you can see my original design of Shep, next to Steve's version. I eventually settled on a mix of the two. I kept the "Michelin Man" body rolls for sound absorption due to Shep's sonic powers. But I loved the "Phantom Cruiser" eyes that Steve added.

▲ My original Shep.



© 2012 Steve Rude

▲ My original inks, with color.

▲ Steve adds shadows.

The depiction of light and shadow is critical for giving characters a sense of solidity and depth. Yet in my initial version of the seated Lamakk there were almost no black shadows at all. My goal in this series was to emulate old animated TV shows as much as possible, and few of them had the luxury to depict shadow in their black line art. In fact, the shows of the mid-sixties weren't even inked. They were produced with a process akin to xeroxed pencil drawings that were painted. So my plan was to provide the tones with color shadows as you see here.

Well, in October of 2012, I visited Steve in Phoenix for a few days to get his feedback on my progress. When I went back to my hotel one night I left my inked line art at his home. The next morning, Steve said, "I hope you don't mind…I took the liberty…", as he handed this page back to me, now beautifully inked.

When Steve drew these drawings above, the justifications for my approach crumbled immediately. Everything just looked so much *better* with shadows. Right then and there I decided not to fanatically try to make my series look *exactly* like the TV shows, but to remember that they are, in fact, *comics*.

I also remembered that with Jonny Quest, Joe Barbera's goal had been to make a *comic book* come to life. When you watch that show you see quite a few scenes that are fully inked with deep black shadows. Though Hanna-Barbera couldn't afford to continue that look, it had been the intention at the outset. And

honestly I never liked the thin-lined, xeroxed pencil look of the animation in the later shows anyway. So my philosophy became, what would the shows have looked like with Joe Barbera's original intent? And a massive budget?

On this page I wanted to show you the remaining images Steve created that found their way into the final art. In most cases they were a much improved take on something I had originally done (as you saw on page 30).

All images this page
© 2012 Steve Rude